CW00865597

ISBN: 9798775469801

DEDICATION

This story is dedicated to Nancy and Betty,
who inspired Tilly's energy, positivity and wisdom.

And to our beloved Fonne,
who was about as far from this Alfonse as it's possible to get.

We miss you, Gramps.

A Hog's Tale.

Words Lori Meakin
Pictures Dave Waters

Sir Alfonse, a privileged,
bossy young hog,
Had gone out for playtime
with Tilly, his dog.

"Let's play hide and seek"
shouted Tilly, delighted.
"Alfonse, can we please?
I would be so excited!"

"Of course not! We have
to play something I choose,"
Said the hog,
and Tilly's tail sank at the news.

Her smile faded too
but she answered "I see."
And Alfonse explained
the way things had to be...

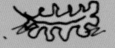

"We'll do just whatever
I say we must do.
It's simple. I'm much more
important than you."
He continued, "I know
that it may not be fair,
But Tilly,
I simply don't care!"

"Now listen," he went on,
"to Alfonse, your master.
I want us to race,
to see who can run faster."

"Fantastic!" said Tilly,
and scampered away.
But Alfonse then shouted
"Oh no, not that way!"

He'd stumbled and fallen
while Tilly was cruising,
And, as he was selfish
and couldn't stand losing,
He leant on a post and cried
"I'm the winner!
That Tilly is rubbish!
I really should bin her!"

"It's my game, and I
am the winner, you see?
No matter that you
can run faster than me.
I make up the rules
as the game goes along.
I'm Alfonse,
and I'm never wrong!"

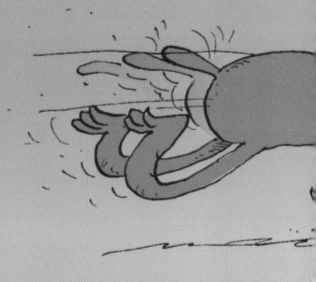

"But come on now Tilly,
let's play something fun,"
Said Alfonse. "since playtime
has barely begun."

They skipped and they hopped
til they came to a wood.
"Watch me" said the hog.
"For I know that we should
Always look after nature
and flowers and trees,
But I simply don't care,
and I do as I please!"

He pulled at the branches
til one of them broke,
And he laughed as if someone
had just told a joke.

"I do what I want 'cause
I'm special, you see.
I don't care for anything
other than me.
I wouldn't feel bad if you
begged on your knees.
I'm Alfonse the Great,
so hard cheese!"

As he finished his speech
he skipped right round the tree.
Then he turned to his dog and said,
"Ooh, I love me!"

But Tilly, who followed
a short way behind,
Said "Alfonse, I'm worried
that wasn't so kind!"

"Be quiet" he shouted,
"for I see a bunny."
His catapult raised, he said,
"This will be funny!"

He fired a stone, then he
laughed and he clapped.
But his joy was short-lived,
for his catapult snapped.

"My catapult's rubbish!
I need something new.
I want to throw stones
and make trouble, it's true.
I'll hurt any bunny
or tree that I see.
I'm Alfonse,
it's all about me!"

Now Tilly looked up at the hog
with a frown,
But Alfonse was shouting
and dancing around:

"I hurt him, I hurt him!
Oh I love this game!
I hit him with stones,
now I'll call him a name!"

"Oh Alfonse, I think you should stop,
that's so mean!"
Cried young Tilly, amazed at
the cruelty she'd seen.

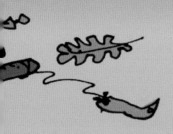

But Alfonse then stopped and cried,
"Oh, I've been cut!"
His head had been hit
by a large falling nut!

"Caruthers! That hurt!
How can something hurt me?
I do what I like
and I'm special, you see.
Who cares about others?
I just love myself,
I'm Alfonse,
with power and wealth."

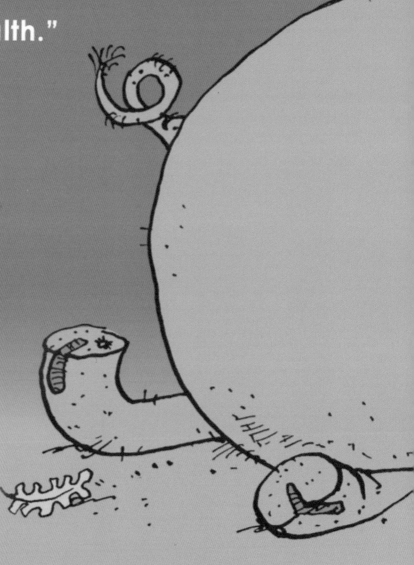

Then Alfonse stood up
and said "Maybe I ought to
Try cleaning my head.
Oh look, here is some water."

He knelt by a poolside,
now feeling quite weak.
And as he bent down
he saw something unique –
The hog in the lake
began talking to him,
A talking reflection,
a magical thing!

A voice like his own
floated up from the lake,
Saying "Here's some advice
that I'd like you to take,"
"Just sit" it continued,
"and listen to me,
And after you've listened
then maybe you'll see."

"I don't want to see"
interrupted the hog,
But then settled himself on a log.

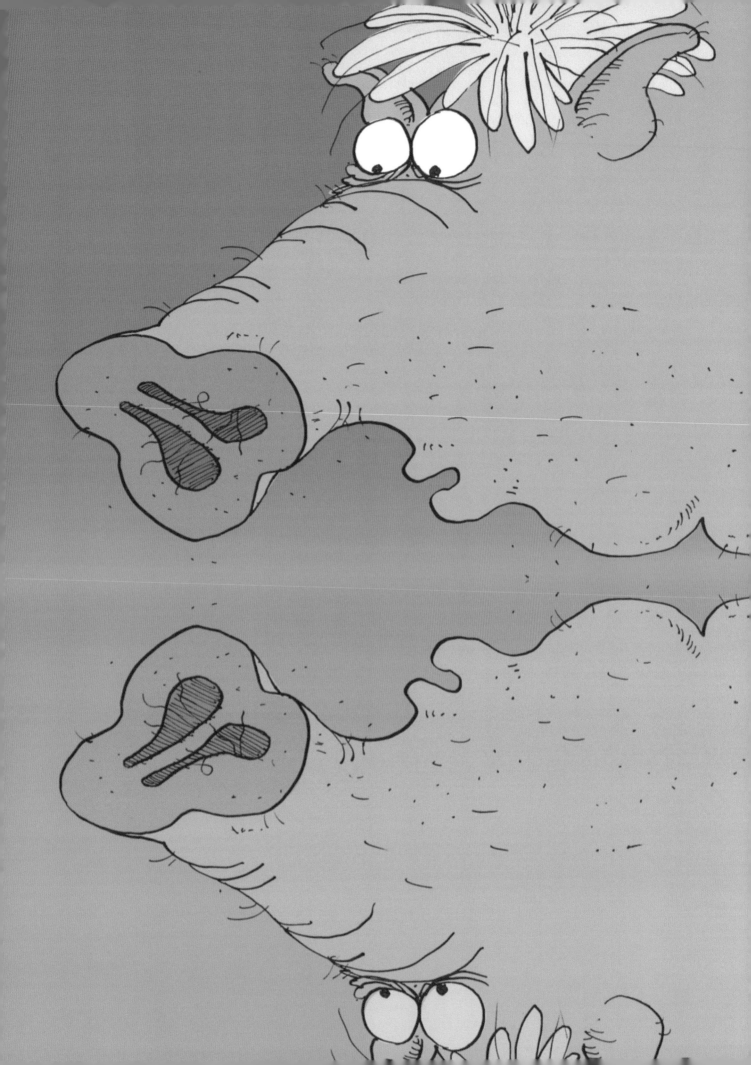

"The things that you do
Come right back at you.
So if you are mean,
Then just as you've seen,
The bad things come back.
You're under attack!
There's no way around it,
It's just as you found it.
But if you could stop,
Go back to the top,
Well then you might see
How else you could be.

You could have been kind,
And then you would find
That kindness would grow
Like a seed that you sow.
Each good thing you do
Would bring good things to you.

Just think about it, and
then give it a go,
Because kindness makes
kindness come back, don't you know."

As Alfonse stood watching
that hog in the pool,
He thought. And he realised
he'd been a fool!

"This 'do unto others
as they do to you',
Or 'Karma,' as some people
call it, is true!
My catapult broke
when I damaged a tree.
When I hurt a rabbit,
a nut then hurt me.

Perhaps I should try out this
'being kind' lark?"
At this, Tilly gave
an encouraging bark...

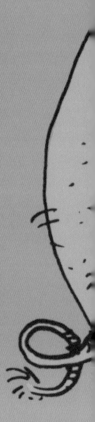

"Oh Alfonse! I see that you're
over your worst.
You'll make sacrifices
and put others first."

"I wouldn't say that!"
said the hog with a grin,
"I'll spread kindness round
so we all get to win.
You might say I'm still being
selfish, you see,
As goodness to others
brings good things to me!"

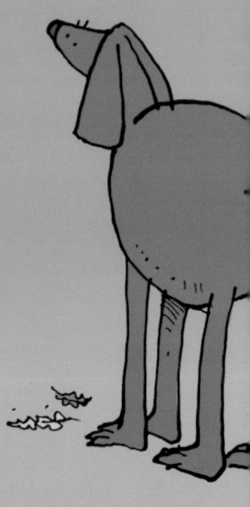

"I see what you mean...
but I don't think we'll mind"
Sighed Tilly, "as long as
you keep being kind"

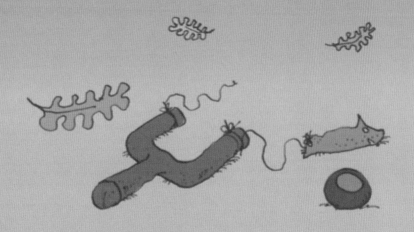

ACKNOWLEDGMENTS

Thanks to Jonny for cooking me wonderful food while I mess around writing.

To Dave for bringing these characters so brilliantly to life.

And to all the family and friends who've told me to get this thing published.

See, I do listen sometimes

xx